Back to School Tortoise

Written by
Lucy M George

Illustrated by
Merel Eyckerman

meadowside 🍃
CHILDREN'S BOOKS

Summer was almost over.

It was time to go
back to school.

He got up,

got dressed,

and had
breakfast.

Then he left
for school.

But he started
thinking,

what if...

...he tripped over?

Or he didn't like lunch?

Or the kids were
mean to him?

What if he tripped
over getting lunch,

and all the kids
were mean to him?

'No,' he decided.
'I can't go in.'

He sat down
by the door.

But then he
started thinking,
what if...

...it was fun?

Or lunch was his favourite?

Or he made lots of new friends?

What if it was fun eating
his favourite lunch,

with all his new friends?

'I'll go to school!' he decided.

He took a
deep breath,

and opened
the door...

'Good morning, everyone!'

Tortoise said, as bravely as he could.

'Good morning, Mr Tortoise!'

they all shouted back.

For Mr and Mrs Andrews

L.M.G.

For everyone!

M.E.

First published in 2010
by Meadowside Children's Books
185 Fleet Street, London, EC4A 2HS

www.meadowsidebooks.com

Text © Lucy M George 2010
Illustrations © Merel Eyckerman 2010

The rights of Lucy M George and Merel Eyckerman
to be identified as the author and illustrator
of this work have been asserted by them in accordance
with the Copyright, Designs and Patents Act, 1988

A CIP catalogue record for this book
is available from the British Library

10 9 8 7 6 5 4 3 2

Printed in China